Christmas greetings
and a happy
2022!

Marilyn Nelson

THE

BAOBAB

ROOM

THE BAOBAB ROOM

BY

Father Jacques de Foïard-Brown
with Marilyn Nelson

LITTLE BOUND BOOKS
A DIVISION OF HOMEBOUND PUBLICATIONS
WWW.LITTLEBOUNDBOOKS.COM

LITTLE BOUND BOOKS
Small Books. Big Impact | www.littleboundbooks.com

Quantity sales. Special discounts are available on quantity purchases by corporations, associations, bookstores and others. For details, contact the publisher or visit wholesalers such as Ingram or Baker & Taylor.

Published in 2019 • Little Bound Books
ISBN • 978-1-947003-53-8
First Edition Hardcover

An Imprint of Homebound Publications
Front Cover Watercolor by © Val_Iva
Interior Illustration (Cat) by © Mika Besfamilnaya
Interior Illustration (Gecko) by © Sliver Kat
All Other Interior Illustrations by © ImHope
Cover and Interior Designed • Leslie M. Browning

Printed in the United States of America
10 9 8 7 6 5 4 3 2 1

Little Bound Books is committed to ecological stewardship. We greatly value the natural environment and invest in environmental conservation.

Abba Jacob is a monk.
He lives alone in a little hermitage
on an island in a far-away sea.
His job is to pray and work,
pray and work all day,
and to welcome visitors.
Once in a great while Abba Jacob
travels across the sea
and gives talks to people
about listening to silence.

On this one particular day,
a group of children ask,
"How did you learn to hear silence?"

Abba Jacob said,
"Where I grew up in Africa,
for some time I lived in an old, old Baobab tree.
There I found my best silence teacher."

The children laughed.
"Were you a monkey then, Abba Jacob,
living up in a tree?"

"And why not?" Abba Jacob asked.
"Am I not sitting here today
with a lot of little monkeys?
Do you think I was not once
a little monkey, myself?

"But I lived not up in,
but inside, my Baobab tree.
Baobab trees grow to be very old,
a thousand years or more, and very large.
All fifteen of you holding hands
with your arms spread wide
would barely make a chain around my tree."

"I've seen a redwood tree that big in California,"
said Mark-David. "It was so tall
you couldn't see the top of it!
Did your Baobab tree look like a redwood?"

Abba Jacob said, "When a Baobab is still young,
a baby of just one or two hundred years,
it is tall and straight just like any other tree,
with shiny leaves, strong branches, and smooth bark.
It is a giddy, a lucky and fine thing to be young,
to have smooth skin, to be all one
even shape, graceful, slim, agile.
You want to grow up, but not too old,
not old enough to be ugly.
Little by little, you realize
that living life to the full, knocks and all,
makes you in the end more beautiful, not less.
Baobab trees show you that.

"As it gets older and fatter,
full of old scars and memories,
each Baobab takes on a shape of its own.
If you befriend a Baobab, you quickly see
that this one is like no other;
you recognize your tree from afar,
a gray, massive form, like a rock,
through the other trees.
As you walk toward your tree
your heart beats faster, you are going
to meet a friend. And a true friend
does not have just an outside,
he has an inside too, no?
Just as we all do.

"As a Baobab's trunk grows outwards,
there is such a lot of it
that there is no need for all of it
to take water to the leaves and sugar to the roots.
The part that is unnecessary is let go.

It becomes a sweet-smelling compost
at the heart of the tree, feeding
all kinds of insects and worms.
After many years there is a hollow,
with a smooth skin on its walls.
In the middle of my Baobab friend
was a hollow large enough for all of us
to sit around its cool, smooth walls
scrunched together like corn kernels on a cob.

"My old friend had a very special inner room,
because a branch had been torn away
in a storm a long, long time ago,
so there was an opening to the light
at the top. You could look up
and see the slow-moving clouds."

"How did you get in?" asked Aisha.

"Someone or something
had made an opening near the ground.
I could just squeeze in.
Perhaps the elephants made it
with their tusks
when they came to tear up the bark
and suck the moisture.
The elephant is the closest thing
in the animal kingdom to the Baobab.
The same massive presence, the same
wrinkled gray skin, the venerable age.

"The elephantlets,
of course, are as scatter-brained
as you lot, and as fun-loving.
I have seen them on a steep, slippery riverbank,
four of them together sliding on their bottoms
down the mudslide, squealing with glee, to land
with a splash in the water and race round
to be the first to start again at the top.

"Or perhaps the doorway was cut in
by the same little Bushmen
who had hammered wooden pegs
in the tree all the way up to the top
to see afar for hunting,
or to get at the fruit or the bees."

Aisha squealed, "Bees?
You mean the kind that sting?"

"Every respectable Baobab has at least
one bee hive. My old friend had two:
one in a big hollow branch, and one
sheltered in the armpit of another branch
at the angle where it joined the trunk.
You could see the big golden combs
filled with honey, and hear the bees
coming and going, yellow African bees,
quite fierce, gleaming like amber beads
in the sunlight. They give you
a good warning buzz
if you get too near.

"I saw the half-Bushman hunters
smoke them out to steal a little honey.
One of them would climb up the tree
with burning smoky straw
and with a cloth around his head,
and smoke the hive, then snatch as much honey
as he could and scramble down and run.

"You're lucky if you get away
with only a few stings. More often
it was many stings. They hurt!

"You could still see the neat row
of holes that remained
from the old Bushmen ladder,
and, right at the top, one rotten old peg still.

"But those little old people were long gone,
I am sorry to say. There was a flat stone
between the great roots, with a small hollow

in the middle, and I found a pebble
a few steps away, round and smooth,
that fit comfortably in my hand, and I knew
the ancient Bushmen had used those two stones
to crush seeds and roots before cooking."

"Who were the Bushmen?" asked Justine.

"The Bushmen, or San, are the original people
of Southern Africa.
They were hunters and gatherers there farther back
than anyone can remember, at least 40,000 years.
They were driven out, first by the Bantu people,
then by the Europeans. There are now only a few
tens of thousands of San Bushmen left,
eking out an existence
on the edges of the Kalahari desert.
They are a slim little people,
with apricot colored skin and tight curly hair.
The rock caves of Southern Africa are filled

to this day with their paintings of animals and people.
They are a gentle people who love song and dancing.
 Sometimes, if I was silent enough in my tree, I thought
I could feel their presence and hear,
like the song of the bees, high voices
carried by the wind from miles away.

"So every visitor left a mark on my tree.
And even with the cutting, the tearing of bark,
the piercing of the trunk, it seemed
there was no complaining, no whining.
The grandfather/mother simply set to work
repairing and healing, and the scars
made it more beautiful."

"More beautiful, Abba?" asked Alex.

"There are different kinds of beauty.
One is the beauty of clear youth,
of regularity, of no fault-lines, no blemishes;

but there is a deeper beauty which comes
from a history, a wisdom, from difficulties
you have overcome, things you have given away,
friendship received, hurts and slights forgiven.
That is your true beauty. The rest is appearance:
it is here one day and gone tomorrow.

"It is a wonderful thing to see
a Baobab become more beautiful.
The Baobab is the greatest tree in its land,
but it has the softest wood,
even though there are strong fibers
from which you can make ropes and mats.
Wherever it is cut, even inside the trunk,
a Baobab grows a skin again, quite smooth,
but often with many knobs and nooks.
If you are always surrounded by walls,
protected by armor, guns, and dogs,
how can you have true friends, do good
to anyone? Perhaps, like our little Bushmen,
you can be too vulnerable, and the powerful

will brush you aside. But what if you do not
take the risk? Taking that risk
is another way to describe compassion,
being sensitive to the sufferings
of others. Then is your own heart
healed from its inner ugliness.

"I have seen bulldozers clearing land
give up the fight every time
against a Baobab. Forest fires
only singe it. It wins
by yielding."

"Were you alone
all the time in your Baobab, Abba?"

"In the beginning I thought I was alone,
and I busied myself cleaning out my house,
climbing up and down outside to and from

my observation point in the sky.
After sitting in the cool shade inside,
coming out to the light was a revelation.
And coming out of the light
into the shade and protection
was a rest for the spirit.
But soon I found I was never alone.
There was the tree, whose presence, whose kindness
said, "I don't do, I don't shout, I am."
And there were all the others, who found there
shelter, space, hiding, food.
If I was quiet like my friend,
they would reveal their presence
and go about their business."

"The others?"

"I have already told you about the bees.
But there were other permanent residents
and quite a few visitors. Perhaps most present

and most quiet during the day were those
who come out at night. A big gray owl
perched at the very top of the chamber.
What eyes!
Regularly there would be a message
from his lordship, a pellet
of compressed fur, quite clean.

"There were the bats
hanging in another corner.
They woke at dusk and flew all night
from tree to tree with their radar on.
I could hear their clicks.
They drank the nectar
from the baobab flowers,
and carried pollen on their fur
like little brown angels delivering kisses.

"A shy dormouse lived in a hole,
where he secreted nuts
and scratched away now and then.

"The geckos would run about
on the walls and cry chick-chack all night.
They come out at dusk to hunt for insects.
They stalk every insect, especially moths,
with great concentration, then there is a swift rush
and the moth is in the gecko's mouth.
The suckers on their feet
mean that they are as comfortable
hanging upside down as right side up.

"I must tell you about a particular
friend. Such a discreet one, I almost
never got to know him.
On a ledge in my Baobab room, I saw
one day out of the corner of my eye
something pale in the deep shade.
I lighted some straw to see more clearly.
I saw a big white frog, the size of my hand,
I had never seen before.
I put out my hand;
he moved back a half-inch,
looking quite unafraid.
So I left him in peace
and always found him there again
during the day, unmoved by any emotion.
He must have given out the word
to his mates because later I found
that several white frogs had taken up residence.

"I saw them come alive at dusk.
What extraordinary athletes they were,
leaping from absolute immobility
to the other side of the room in one jump,
to cling to a tiny ledge on the wall,
on the lookout for insects,
back to their inscrutable pose.
They were giant white tree-frogs.

"But where did they come from?
That is still a mystery to me.
Frogs need water to breed. Perhaps
they bred in the holes on top of the tree
which collected water during the rains?

"But though I saw those tree-puddles
mobbed by bees coming to drink,
I never saw any tadpoles. Perhaps
 the giant white tree-frog has a great secret.
But who does not?

"There were many birds.
In the summer a red-breasted swallow
would make her clay nest with a long entrance,
under a branch like the hive
but on the other side of the tree.
I could hear the loud twittering of the chicks
when the parents flew in with full beaks.

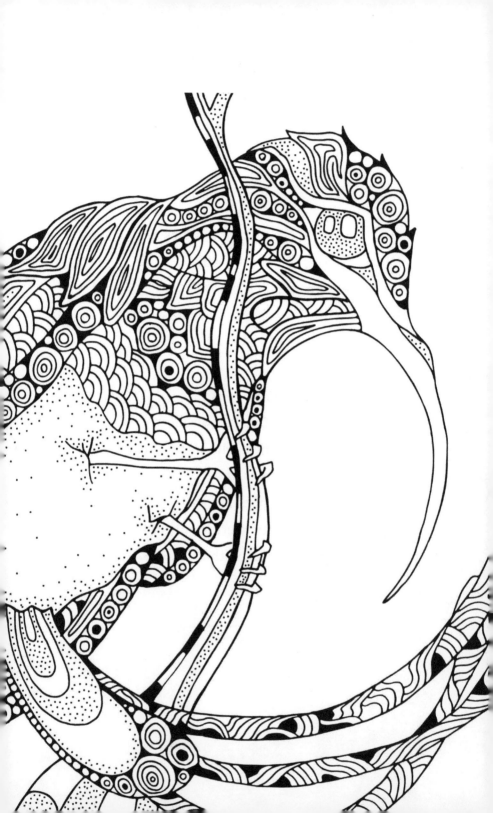

"Other birds came and went:
the hammercrop, a large ungainly brown bird
with a crested head like a hammer and a nest
in the center of a huge bundle of twigs;
the turtle doves;
the drongoes in black and forked tail;
the bee-eaters resplendent in carmine
or green and turquoise; the paradise fly-catcher
with its long green tail-feathers, darting
in and out of the leaves; the odd eagle and hawk
coming to perch up top and ruffle its feathers and clack
its beak. You could hear the guinea-fowl
from far as they came in a flock chattering
and scratching away. They always left
a few polka-dot feathers in the sand—
more than a few, if the hawk pounced on one.

"The porcupine was a regular visitor.
He would also regularly leave
his visiting cards, fine quills,
black and white, that you can stick into a cork
and use as a float for fishing.

"Then tracks. The cobra came:

I saw his zig-zags in the sand. Or waves,

the tracks of the hooded cobra, Pharaoh.

At home I would kill them: that was my job,

for they ate Mama's chickens, struck at the dogs,

and sowed panic everywhere.

Their cousin the spitting cobra spits

in the eye; I had to take him out from afar

bazooka style, with the long hippo-hide whip

my father made for me.

"In the Baobab we made a truce,
we signed a pact of non-aggression.
Someone had to keep down the mice
apart from Owl. Besides,
I rather like snakes.
Don't you admire them, too, a little?

"Oh!
The bushbuck has passed,
elegant he, with his lyre horns!
And the duiker antelope, hardly bigger
than a terrier: look at the little hooves,
the liquid eyes. They complain
in the village, and call her
a gobbler of salad.
'Who, me?' Don't give me
that innocent look, lady.
You left your hoof-prints
in the garden for everyone to see.

"The room sometimes smells
of the Genet cat, who wears a yellow
robe camouflaged with black:
wicked, but so handsome his beauty
almost makes you faint.

"I hope he has not eaten Frog.
No, there he is.
No pushover, Frog.
I suspect he (or is it she?)
goes invisible at will.
Come on, Frog, tell us your secret!

"This is sandstone country,
and the fine Kalahari sand
has been blown here from the desert.
I dig my bare feet into the red sand
and sit against the silver-gray roots.
I become a tree, not any tree,
but this wise old one.

"I feel close to every tree, to everyone
who ever leaned upon a tree.
I can lean back and look straight up
at the dome of leaves, hand sized,
boat shaped, pale green,
into which the great branches vanish.
This is the dry season,
not a cloud in the blue surround.

"There is still fruit
inside the parasol canopy
even though the vervet monkeys and baboons
have stopped by more than once.

"All animals like the tart taste
when they can break the fruit open.
I have one in my hand now, the size
of a big apple but egg-shaped.

"It is really hard to break,
the only thing that is hard
about the Baobab.
But it is covered in warm
olive-green velvet.
You'd feel like taking it to bed
and putting it under your pillow
(I do that sometimes).
There is a faint musty smell.
This one I crack
with the Bushman stone
on the mortar slab in the hollow.
Several sharp blows,
and it cracks open. Pow!
There is a white powdery paste
with black seeds the size of fingernails.

"The powder has a sharp sour taste.
I am told that it is full of vitamin C.
Time to put some away for the next safari!

"As if summoned by the opened pod,
the Meercat tribe arrives.
Meercats always appear uninvited,
when there is something to scrounge.
They are not cats at all, of course,
but a kind of mongoose which live
in little communities in the dry bushlands and hills.
Fearless, cheeky little animals they are,
but not foolish. There is always a sentinel
to warn when he sees the swooping eagle,
or sees the tip of a cat's tail swish.
They will eat anything and scurry about
searching every possible hiding place for insects and seeds.

"Now and then they get up on their hind feet
to have a look around. They know me by now,
and keep a polite distance of about three feet.
They accept an offer of the other half of the fruit.
Then, whistle! They go into their holes:
a Bateleur eagle is gliding past.
How is it they have all
become family to me here at the Baobab tree?

"But I am suddenly hungry.
Mama has packed some boiled corn cobs in my bag,
just in case the great hunter is unlucky today.
Would you like to share?

"It is very warm, so I will go inside now,
to listen to silence."
Abba Jacob looked around the circle.

Then he sat up straighter,
took a deep breath, and closed his eyes.
The children were quiet, waiting.
Waiting...

"Abba! Where are you? Come back!
Tell us about the magic!
You were going to teach us how to hear silence!"

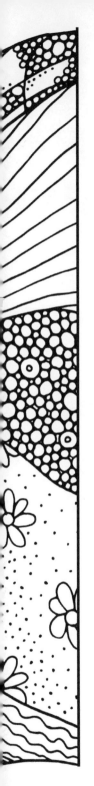

Abba Jacob opened his eyes and smiled.
"What else have I been doing,
you little knuckleheads?
I don't want to disappoint you, but
for the magic of things there is no need
for secret formulas, incantations, witches' brew.
True magic is about letting go
of the appearance of things,
the noise and movements they make,
and reaching for the magical inside.
Hearing silence is about listening to silence,
taking in the magic of being.

37

"You have to go to that inner
vulnerable space,
where someone greater than you
will reach for you in friendship.
We find magic by coming awake deeper,
in our center, in our heart.
Be like the Baobab, vulnerable.
Make space at your core
for someone who loves you very much.
Remain with that love in silence
and all is well with you.
Nothing is a stranger to you
in your Baobab room.

"Let's be quiet now, and see
if you can hear."

Abba Jacob, then the children,
closed their eyes and listened.

"Oh, I hear!" cried Jonathan.
"There's a song in the silence!"

Father Jacques de Foïard-Brown

Father Jacques de Foïard-Brown of Mauritius leads retreats and conferences in France and elsewhere. He spent part of his boyhood in Zimbabwe, after which he was trained at the University of California, Davis as an agronomist and received a post-graduate degree in developmental economics at Cambridge University. He received God's call one day and entered the Benedictine monastery of Solesmes in France, where he remained for seven years. Returning to his country of origin, he was ordained a priest and a teacher of Christian meditation. He has lived in a hermitage for almost forty years, while serving the communities that surround it. *The Baobab Room* is his first book.

Marilyn Nelson

Marilyn Nelson is the author or translator of more than twenty critically acclaimed books for adults and children, and the recipient of many honors and awards, including the Frost Medal, the Golden Rose Award, the NSK Neustadt Award, and the NCTE Poetry Award. She has served as a Chancellor of the Academy of American Poets, as Poet-In-Residence of the Cathedral of St. John the Divine, and as Poet Laureate of Connecticut. Father Jacques appears, disguised as "Abba Jacob," in several of her books.

Marilyn Nelson and Jacques Brown met at a party as undergraduate students in 1966.

LITTLE
BOUND BOOKS

OTHER OFFERINGS TO CONSIDER

Naming the Unnameable by Dr. Rev. Matthew Fox

Companions on the Way by Gunilla Norris

Listen by Francesca G. Varela

To Lose the Madness by L.M. Browning

A Comet's Tail by Amy Nawrocki

A Fistful of Stars by Gail Collins-Ranadive

A Letter to My Daughters by Theodore Richards

Terranexus by David K. Leff

What Comes Next by Heidi Barr

Great Pan is Dead by Eric D. Lehman

How Dams Fall by Will Falk

Falling Up by Scott Edward Anderson

WWW.LITTLEBOUNDBOOKS.COM

LOOK FOR OUR TITLES WHEREVER BOOKS ARE SOLD

CPSIA information can be obtained
at www.ICGtesting.com
Printed in the USA
LVHW111957060919
630220LV00001B/1/P